dick bruna

miffy
the fairy

TED SMART

Oh, Miffy sighed, a fairy,

that's what I'd like to be,

and then I could do magic,

oh, what a thrill for me!

My house is really rather small

for fairies, at the least,

it might be good to start just here,

I think that would be best.

The picture shows you what I do,

I wave my wand, and when

I've said: hey presto! I just wait

to see what happens then.

Oh look, there is a castle now

where my house used to stand,

so fine, in yellow, red and blue,

oh, what could be more grand!

And do you see that little bird,

that bird feels very sad,

he says he'd really like a tail –

to have no tail is bad.

Then I say: I'm a fairy,

just see what I can do,

I wave my wand – he has a tail!

Red, yellow, green and blue.

And look at that frog over there,

that frog does not look glad,

if your head was as bald as mine,

he says, then you'd be sad.

To put a crown on his bald head

I simply wave my wand,

and then he looks quite different

he's smiling in the pond.

So when I wave my magic wand,

some happiness you see,

but now and then I help myself

and that is great for me.

So if, down in the garden,

a yellow pear I see,

then I will wave my wand and hang

some apples on the tree.

The pear tree's now an apple tree

with apples red and round,

they taste so nice, and better still

they're good for you, I've found.

To be a magic fairy

that really would be fun,

for she could do so much, much more

than me, plain Miffy bun.

miffy's library

"nijntje de toverfee"
Produced in Great Britain 2006 for The Book People Ltd, Hall Wood Avenue,
Haydock, St Helens WA11 9UL by Egmont UK Limited, 239 Kensington
High Street, London W8 6SA.
Publication licensed by Mercis Publishing bv, Amsterdam
Original text Dick Bruna © copyright Mercis Publishing bv, 2001
Illustrations Dick Bruna © copyright Mercis bv, 2001
Original English translation © copyright Patricia Crampton, 2001
The moral right of the author has been asserted.
Printed in China
10 9 8 7 6 5 4 3 2 1